This Little Tiger book belongs to:

_____

_____

THE BEAR STYLIST

For Steven Lenton. Here's to lots
of salmon sandwiches – SB

For Sharon and love,
wherever it be found – JS

STRIPES PUBLISHING LIMITED
An imprint of the Little Tiger Group
1 Coda Studios, 189 Munster Road, London SW6 6AW

Imported into the EEA by Penguin Random House Ireland,
Morrison Chambers, 32 Nassau Street, Dublin D02 YH68

First published in Great Britain in 2022

ISBN: 978-1-78895-252-1

Printed and bound in China.

STP/3800/0448/1121

The Forest Stewardship Council® (FSC®) is a global, not-for-profit organization dedicated
to the promotion of responsible forest management worldwide. FSC defines standards
based on agreed principles for responsible forest stewardship that are supported by
environmental, social, and economic stakeholders. To learn more, visit www.fsc.org

2 4 6 8 10 9 7 5 3 1

THE BEAR STYLIST

Steven Butler

Illustrated by Jacob Souva

LITTLE TIGER
LONDON

CHAPTER 1

DING! DING! DING!

At 6:30am exactly, Ludo P. Tubbs climbed out of bed, tried to touch his toes, failed to touch his toes, then *rushed* around his den getting ready for another busy day.

The little bear took his
usual super soapy shower
using his homemade
shiny-do-shampoo.

Then he floofed his
eyebrows, scrubbed
his claws and combed
every patch of fur to
get rid of any stray
fleas or ticks.

Next Ludo put on his shirt, waistcoat and tie, and looked at himself in the mirror. Everything had to be neat and perfect. You see, Ludo was a bear stylist – and not just any bear stylist. The Tubbs of Crooked Mountain had been the most famous bear-dressing family for as long as anyone could remember.

Ludo's dad was a bear stylist and *his* mum and *her* dad and *his* aunt and *her* gran ... all the way back to Great–Great–Great–Great Uncle Tobias Tubbs. True and reliable, and always sticking to the rules of the

BEAR-DRESSER'S CODE:

Listen to your customers and only give them the exact cut they ask for!

When Ludo checked his pocket watch, it was 6:59am. Perfect timing, as always. He grabbed his bear-stylist's bag, picked up his list of customers and tucked it into his waistcoat pocket. He then hopped on to his trusty old bicycle with the rusty front-wheel and squeaked off into the woods.

Ludo's first stop was the warren of Beverly Hopkins and her children: Fluffy, Wuffy, Huffy, Stuffy, Muffy, Guffy, Tuffy, Ruffy, Bluffy, Duffy, Juffy, Puffy, Zuffy and Tallulah.

Any other bear-dresser would have run away at the sight of so many wriggling toddlers in need of a trim but not Ludo. Inside his AMAZING bear-stylist's bag was a gadget for every occasion. While Mrs Hopkins relaxed and got a perm, the multi-snip-o-matic made light work of her fourteen children.

"Oh, they look lovely! And my perm is perfect!" Mrs Hopkins beamed as she paid Ludo with a jar of carrot chutney. "You're a marvel!"

Ludo nodded a thank you. He was a bear of few words, so he opted for a cheerful smile and a wave as he set off again on his bicycle.

The next customer of the morning was Horacio Bushwinkle at the top of the ancient oak.

Once he'd squished inside, Ludo set about quietly curling Mr Bushwinkle's ear-tufts and crimping his bushy tail with his handy squirrelizer.

"Top notch!" Mr Bushwinkle cooed as
he paid Ludo with a slice of acorn paté.
"My bristles are **BRILLIANT!**"

In no time Ludo was back on his trusty bicycle, **huffing** and **puffing** up the slopes of Crooked Mountain to visit Machu and Picchu.

The alpaca twins always liked to look exactly
the same but today there was a problem.
Machu wanted long twisty braids to swing
around her shoulders and Picchu wanted
buns on the top of her head.

Ludo thought for a moment, then pulled out his braid-and-bun-a-ma-bob.

"Problem solved!" the twins whooped as they paid Ludo three balls of alpaca-hair wool. "We are braided bunly beauties!"

Gregory Clawson was thrilled with his fancy mane,

Professor Phi Phi Canard quacked so loudly when she saw her reflection she almost fell into the pond

and Mama Stripe felt like a brand-new zebra with her snazzy blond bob.

The sun started to set but Ludo wasn't even close to finishing his work. He just had time to gobble down one of the salmon sandwiches he'd packed that morning, before pedalling off to see his nocturnal customers.

Herbert Snuffler wanted his grey streaks dyed black to impress the lady–badger next door. "It's gone white here and here … and here!" he sighed. "Oh, I'm getting old."

Amelia Grubble the bandicoot had her whiskers waxed and the McFlop family needed their snouts shampooed.
The bats refused to fly down from their precarious perches but Ludo didn't mind.
It was all in a day's … no, a night's work.

By the time he got back to his den, the sun was already peeking over Crooked Mountain. Ludo folded his clothes, climbed into bed and fell fast aslee– zzzzzzzzzzzzzzzzzzzzzz

But not for long...

DING! DING! DING!

CHAPTER 2

Ludo showered and dressed and hopped on his bicycle. Still yawning and rubbing his eyes, he pedalled off to visit the first customer on today's list – Reginald Scrunch. The little bear knocked on his door and...

He gasped as the doddery aardvark skittered on to the front step of his burrow sporting an enormous yellow quiff!

"Oh, Ludo," Mr Scrunch said, looking embarrassed. "Sorry, m'bear, I won't be needing you today. That new fellow knocked first thing this morning and I've been primped by him for a change. Marvellous bear-dresser, he is."

Ludo's eyes widened. New bear-dresser? What new bear-dresser?

Mr Scrunch spotted Ludo's confused expression and handed him a small card, then wobbled back inside.

Ludo read it with trembling paws:

Leonardo Van Cropsalot:
Bear Stylist Extraordinaire!

Who could this mystery stranger be?

Ludo hopped on to his bicycle and squeaked off in search of answers.

Before long he passed a bison with a rainbow Mohican. A little while later he spotted a kangaroo with a huge Afro of bright pink curls. Ludo definitely hadn't styled either of *those* animals and a nervous gloopy feeling bubbled up inside his belly.

"Come one! Come all!"

a voice suddenly clamoured through the
trees. Ludo swerved in surprise and crashed
into a bramble bush, sending his bike flying.

As he wriggled free, Ludo spotted a brilliantly
painted wagon at the bottom of the hill.
A crowd of animals was gathered around it
and standing on top, brandishing a comb,
was an enormous bear with the curliest
moustache Ludo had EVER seen.

"Come see my creations!" the bear hollered. "You won't believe your eyes!"

The stranger was right. Ludo didn't believe his eyes. He crept down the hill and gawped at the bear in his sea-green suit.

"I am Leonardo Van Cropsalot and I've come to fulfil your bear-do-dreams.

Who wants to go first?"

Ludo watched as every paw, wing and hoof shot into the air.

"ME! ME! ME!" the animals all howled and grunted.

Ludo's jaw nearly hit the ground when Beverly Hopkins bounded up on to the wagon. He'd only given her a perm yesterday! Had she forgotten?

"My haircut is too boring!" she declared. "I want something with extra glitzy-glamour like those wild rabbits on the telly."

A pang of sadness prickled in Ludo's belly as he watched Leonardo escort Beverly Hopkins to his styling chair. It was covered in gadgets and looked very impressive.

With a *swoosh* and a **FLIP** and a **flop** and a *snip*, Mrs Hopkins' perm was transformed into a towering blue sailing ship.

"Ta-da!" Leonardo roared as the crowd clapped and whooped.

Ludo didn't understand. Mrs Hopkins hadn't asked for a boat-shaped bouffant. Why was she so happy?

The little bear plodded back to his bicycle, feeling extremely glum. How could he compete against a bear like that?

Pulling out his list of customers, Ludo saw his next appointment was with Mrs Maaaa. She'd only want her fleece untangling and that's exactly what he would do. There was NO WAY Ludo was going to break the **BEAR-DRESSER'S CODE**.

"Just a spot of neatening please, deary."

Mrs Maaaa sat in her armchair sipping a cup of tea, while Ludo got stuck in with his brush. Soon the old sheep's fleece was looking tidy and sensible.

Ludo sighed. Tidy and sensible? It suddenly felt very boring indeed.

He was about to pack up when a strange
thought crept into his mind. Before he knew
what he'd done, Ludo raised his scissors and...

Mrs Maaaa didn't seem to have noticed,
so Ludo took another snip and another.
That felt good!

Ludo reached into his bear-stylist's bag and grabbed a pawful of gizmos. In seconds he was

crimping and twisting,

dyeing and waving,

curling and combing.

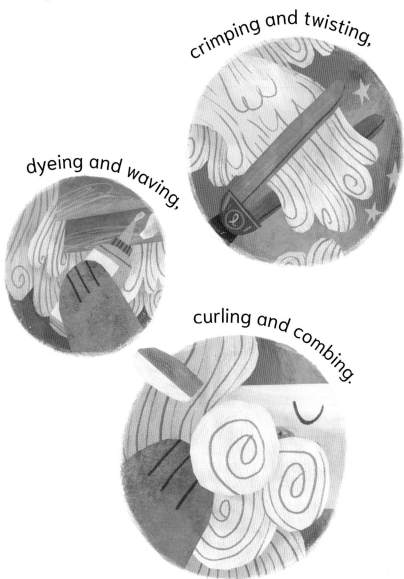

With a final flourish, Ludo picked up his little round mirror and handed it to Mrs Maaaa.

"Oh, are you finished?" she bleated. She held up the mirror and looked at her reflection. **"MAAAAAAAAAAAAAAAGGGGHHHHHH!"**

Ludo suddenly felt sick and his belly gurgled nervously. What had he done? How could he break the **BEAR-DRESSER'S CODE**? He'd ruined this nice old sheep's hairdo and...

"IT'S WONDERFUL!" Mrs Maaaa hopped about, waving her walking stick in the air.

Ludo froze. What did she just say?

"Oh, it's the most magnificent thing I've ever seen. I look like a queen!"

Had Ludo not been covered in fur, Mrs Maaaa would have noticed the little bear blushing like a tomato. The nervous gloopy feeling in his belly was replaced with the biggest bungliest beaming ever.

Ludo packed up, stepped outside into the sunshine and smiled to himself. Maybe Leonardo Van Cropsalot wasn't such a threat after all?

CHAPTER 3

Over the next few days as he pedalled around Crooked Mountain handing out little cards of his own, Ludo spotted Leonardo whizzing about on his turbo-charged scooter. He also saw the odd animal sporting a bright green bear-style in the shape of a palm tree or orange braids going all the way down to the ground.

But that didn't worry Ludo any more.

Not even a tiny bit!

While the big bear scooted back and forth, making towering top-knots and tangled twists, Ludo created new, impressive styles for *his* customers.

Ludo P. Tubbs:
Bear Stylist
EXTRA-EXTRAORDINAIRE!

He was getting braver and more inventive with every snip. Leonardo had even been overheard grumbling about his rival as he zipped around the wood.

Before long, every animal was gossiping about who they were going to get their hair quiffed and quaffed by next.

Ludo was thrilled with Professor Phi Phi
Canard's shock of violet and pink feathers...

...until he saw what wonders Leonardo had
worked on Herbert Snuffler's dreadlocks.

Leonardo went around boasting about
Horacio Bushwinkle's funky new mullet...

...until he saw the amazing work Ludo had
done on Gregory Clawson's spiky mane.

On and on it went, until the morning Ludo
was called to Mayor Munch's mansion.
He was balancing at the top of his ladder,
tending to the giraffe's tallest tufts when...

KNOCK!

KNOCK!

KNOCK!

"Good morning," the mayor said as Leonardo clomped inside. "I forgot you were coming. I hope you don't mind but I've decided to go with Ludo instead. What do you think?"

The huge bear looked like smoke was about to come billowing out of his ears.

"It's **TERRIBLE!**" Leonardo bawled. "Rubbisher than rubbish! You should've waited for **ME!**"

"Come now, Mr Cropsalot! What nonsense!"
Mayor Munch said, glancing at herself in the
mirror. "Ludo has done a splendid job.
I hardly think this is the time for rudeness!"

"But I'm much better than that little squirt!"
Leonardo roared, stamping his paws. "There's
only room for one bear stylist on Crooked
Mountain and I'm it!"

Ludo gave a little **GROWL**.

"That's quite enough!" the mayor snapped.
"I won't have bears fighting in my house like
a pack of humans!"

The giraffe looked up at Ludo, then down at
Leonardo.

"I think this calls for a competition," she said.

"A what?" Leonardo asked.

"A bear–styling competition," the Mayor replied. "Whoever wins will be crowned **BEAR STYLIST SUPREME!**"

Leonardo glared at Ludo. Ludo glared at Leonardo. Finally both bears nodded.

CHAPTER 4

The following weekend, the animals of Crooked Mountain gathered on the lawn outside Mayor Munch's mansion. A stage had been built and everyone crowded around it, wriggling and shoving to get to the front.

The crowd fell silent as Mayor Munch stepped up on to the stage followed by Ludo and Leonardo, dressed in their snazziest suits.

"It is with great excitement that I'm here to judge the **BEAR STYLIST SUPREME** competition," the mayor announced. "The winner gets this TERRIFIC trophy and a year's supply of salmon sandwiches!"

Ludo felt a tingle of nervousness from the top of his ears to the end of his stumpy tail. This was his moment to prove that the Tubbs of Crooked Mountain were the best bear-dressing family in the world. No matter what, he HAD to win.

"Right," Mayor Munch said. "Let's get this competition started with the speed test. Ready ... steady ... GO!"

The bears jumped into action, styling Machu and Picchu. Both bears were a blur of cutting and washing, snipping and drying, clipping and dyeing.

Ludo twisted Machu's braids into the shape of a fish squirting water, while Leonardo styled Picchu's buns into the wings of a ginormous butterfly.

"Time's up!" said the mayor, trotting back on stage to inspect the models. "You've both done a tremendous job, but I think Ludo won that round!"

"That's not fair!" Leonardo roared. "I can do better!"

For their second test, the bears had to work with tiny tweezers as they made-over Mr and Mrs Fuzzle.

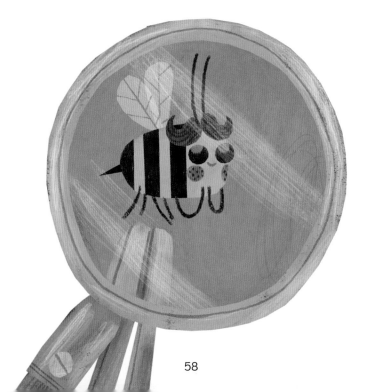

Ludo was delighted with his tiny creation.
Mrs Fuzzle had never looked so gorgeous.
But his heart sank when he saw how dapper
Mr Fuzzle looked with Leonardo's FABULOUS
bumblebee barbering.

"Leonardo wins!" cried the mayor, peering at
the bees through her magnifying glass.

"I WANT A BIGGER CHALLENGE!"

the huge bear hollered.

"You want a challenge, then you've got it!"
said the mayor, dividing the Hopkins children
into two groups. "Your job is to cut their hair
all at the same time without ANY GADGETS!
Your time starts **NOW!**"

Ludo groaned as little rabbits toddled this way and that. If only he could use his multi-snip-o-matic!

He clipped the ends of Fluffy's whiskers with one paw, while shampooing Wuffy's ears with the other. Then curled Huffy's pom-pom tail and plaited patterns into a wriggling Stuffy's back. Just Puffy, Zuffy and Tallulah to go...

"You've got one minute!" shouted Mayor Munch.

Glancing over at Leonardo, Ludo could see that he was having just as much trouble.

61

CRASH!

PING!

WAAAAAHHH!

Leonardo's chair fell off the stage just as Ludo
tripped over a stray tub of fur-wax. Meanwhile,
Puffy covered the crowd with talcum powder,
Zuffy threw the **BEAR STYLIST SUPREME**
trophy into a nearby pond and poor little
Tallulah burst out crying.

"ENOUGH!"

the mayor cried.

Ludo opened one eye, uncurled himself
and slowly stood up.

Nobody made a sound. Until...

"WHAT HAVE YOU DONE?" Beverly

Hopkins shrieked. "Just look at my babies!"

Ludo turned and let out a yelp as he saw

the fourteen Hopkins children.

"I can't believe it!"
Gregory Clawson huffed.

"This is the worst bear-styling
I've EVER seen!" Horacio
Bushwinkle grumbled.

"I'll never get my fleece
plumped by you again!" Mrs
Maaaa bleated.

"So, who won?"
Herbert Snuffler asked.

Everyone looked at Mayor Munch, who had a blob of shaving foam on the top of her head like a squidgy hat.

"No one has won!" she said crossly. "If there can only be one bear stylist on Crooked Mountain, I'm not sure it should be either of YOU!"

Ludo looked sadly at Leonardo. Leonardo looked sadly at Ludo. Then both bears turned and plodded away in opposite directions.

CHAPTER 5

The next day, Ludo's alarm clock went off at 6:30am but he didn't get out of bed.

He'd never felt so down in the dumps in all his life. What would his ancestors think if they could see him now? The Tubbs of Crooked Mountain were supposed to abide by the **BEAR-DRESSER'S CODE** ... not act like clowns.

Ludo didn't bother to have a shower or to put on his shirt, waistcoat and tie. He couldn't even bring himself to eat any breakfast.

Lunchtime rolled around but Ludo couldn't eat his salmon sandwiches.

Evening came but he wasn't in the mood to read a book, or knit some socks, or go for a walk.

He was just thinking about going to bed when there was a knock at the front door.

Ludo opened it and gasped. Standing on the front step was a wet and bedraggled Leonardo.

"Hello," the big bear said, shuffling from foot to foot.

Ludo stared, feeling a little worried.

"I found this in the pond..." Leonardo said. He pulled out his arm from behind his back to reveal the **BEAR STYLIST SUPREME** trophy. "I think you should have it."

Ludo glanced up at Leonardo and smiled.

"W ... w ... w..." he stammered shyly. "Would you like to come in?"

"I thought your bear-styles were marvellous,"
Leonardo said as he sat down on the sofa.
"I'm sorry I didn't tell you before. That was
silly of me."

"I'm sorry too," Ludo said. He smiled again
and offered the big bear a cup of tea.
"This will warm your paws."

GURRRGGRRRGGRRRGGLE! Leonardo's stomach grumbled loudly.

"I didn't feel like eating earlier but now I'm starving!" he admitted.

BLUBBLUBBLUBBLUBBLE! Ludo's tummy growled noisily as well.

After a feast of salmon sandwiches, the bears chatted long into the night. It turned out they both loved adventure books and knitting socks, crunching dry leaves under their paws and snaffling crumbs from the bottom of the biscuit tin.

Leonardo gave Ludo a special ear massage he'd learned when he'd visited the other side of the mountain. Ludo showed Leonardo his great grandmother Grizzle Tubbs' secret recipe for shiny-do-shampoo.

"I… I don't suppose…" the big bear said, wiping his soggy fur out of his eyes. "I don't suppose you could give me a trim, Ludo?"

"I'd be delighted," said the little bear.

The following morning, the animals of Crooked Mountain were woken by a loud commotion.

"What's all that racket?" Mrs Maaaa muttered, peering out of her front door.

"Who's hammering at this early hour?" moaned Herbert Snuffler.

More and more animals came out of their houses and were astonished to discover a large peacock-blue sign above Ludo's door:

Two very snappily dressed bears stepped out sporting AMAZING new bear-styles.

"Me and Leonardo have decided it's much more fun being partners than rivals," Ludo announced.

"Yes," added Leonardo. "No more competing! JUST LOTS OF TERRIFIC BEAR-DOS!"

That was that. The One Stop Crop Shop was a huge success. Animals came from all over Crooked Mountain and beyond to get their **FABULOUS** bear-cuts.

Ludo washed and snipped and curled.

Leonardo clipped and dyed and twirled...

And they both ate salmon sandwiches together until they were very, very old.

THE END

COLLECTIBLE STORIES
WITH COLOUR ILLUSTRATIONS